THIS WALKER BOOK BELONGS TO:

_____

_____

_____

For Michael my Superhero & anyone out in the cold.

First published 2005 by Walker Books Ltd
87 Vauxhall Walk, London SE11 5HJ

This edition published 2006

10 9 8 7 6 5 4 3 2 1

© 2005 Madeleine Floyd

The right of Madeleine Floyd to be identified as author/illustrator
of this work has been asserted by her in accordance with the
Copyright, Designs and Patents Act 1988

This book has been typeset in Godlike Emboldened

Printed in China

British Library Cataloguing in Publication Data: a catalogue record
for this book is available from the British Library

ISBN-13: 978-1-4063-0190-8
ISBN-10: 1-4063-0190-6

www.walkerbooks.co.uk

Cold Paws,
Warm Heart

Madeleine Floyd

WALKER BOOKS
AND SUBSIDIARIES
LONDON · BOSTON · SYDNEY · AUCKLAND

Far away, all alone in the land of snow and ice,
lived a large polar bear who was always cold.
His name was Cold Paws.

When he was young, Cold
Paws tried to play with
the other animals

but he was too big for their games and no one
wanted to play with him.

Soon he started to
feel cold inside.

Poor Cold Paws,
he was very lonely
and he sat on
his own and
shivered.

Time passed slowly for Cold Paws.
The only thing that kept him
company was a silver flute,
which he played each day to
forget his troubles.

Also in the land of snow and ice
there lived a little girl called Hannah.

One day as Hannah was walking through the
forest she heard some beautiful music. She felt
as if the gentle notes were stroking her ears.

The people in the village said that no one lived
across the snowy plains except Cold Paws,
a bear so huge and so cold that if you touched
him you would turn to ice.

But as she closed her eyes in bed that night
all Hannah could think of was the beautiful music.
She knew she would have to follow it.

The next day Hannah took the same path through the snow.

It led her out of the great forest, across the snowy plains

Again she heard the magical music drawing her closer.

and right up to a large iceberg.

Hannah crept towards the iceberg
and peered around the corner.
Right there in front of her was a huge
polar bear with a soft gentle smile.
He was playing a silver flute.

Hannah could not believe her eyes.
She crouched down out of sight
and listened until the air
fell silent around her.

"Brrrrrrrrrrrrrrrrrrrrrrrrrr,"
the polar bear shivered. His whole
body shook and the snow beneath
Hannah's boots trembled.

Now Hannah knew how miserable it was
to feel very cold, so without thinking she took
off her scarf, stepped forward and placed it
right in front of the big polar bear!

Hannah held her breath.

Very slowly the polar bear picked up
the red woolly scarf and tied it under his big
furry chin. He nodded his large heavy head.

Hannah smiled.

That night as the stars lit up the sky, Cold Paws thought how lonely his life had become. He pulled the red scarf closer around his neck but he still felt cold inside.

"Brrrrrrrrrrrrrrrrr,"

he shivered.

On the other side of the forest, Hannah lay in her warm bed and thought about the cold polar bear.

The next day Hannah ran
back through the forest,
across the snowy plains and
up to the iceberg.

"Let's do some star jumps to
warm you up," she said.

Cold Paws looked confused and rubbed his ears. Something about the little girl made him feel better, so he lifted his heavy legs and did his best to jump up and down.

Hannah laughed and Cold Paws smiled.

"I have another idea," said Hannah and she ran off towards the village.

As Cold Paws waited, the sunlight
faded and the snow fell steadily
through the silence. Cold Paws blew
on his polar bear paws. He had never
had such a special day but he still
felt a little cold inside.

"Brrrrrrrrr,"

he shivered.

When Hannah came back she held
out a steaming mug of hot chocolate.
"This is for you," she said.

Cold Paws took the mug in his soft
paws and smelt the sweet chocolate.
He took a large gulp and licked
the chocolate off his nose.

He had never tasted
anything so delicious
and now he only felt
a tiny bit cold inside.

"I have to go home now," said Hannah.
"I can't think of any other way to warm you
up but we can still play together every day."

Hannah reached out her arms as wide as
she could and gave Cold Paws a very big hug.
Cold Paws closed his eyes and as he did so
a wonderful thing happened. The cold feeling
inside disappeared and instead he felt
a warm glow all over.

Now that he had a friend, Cold Paws
didn't feel cold any more.

WALKER BOOKS is the world's leading
independent publisher of children's books.
Working with the best authors and illustrators
we create books for all ages, from babies
to teenagers – books your child will
grow up with and always remember. So…

FOR THE BEST CHILDREN'S BOOKS,
LOOK FOR THE BEAR